LOONS PLANET

Written & Illustrated

HAYLEY FURMAN

A Children's Story Book

CREATED IN DECEMBER 2019

A little time ago, this was my homes view.

I lived here with my family and neighbors too.

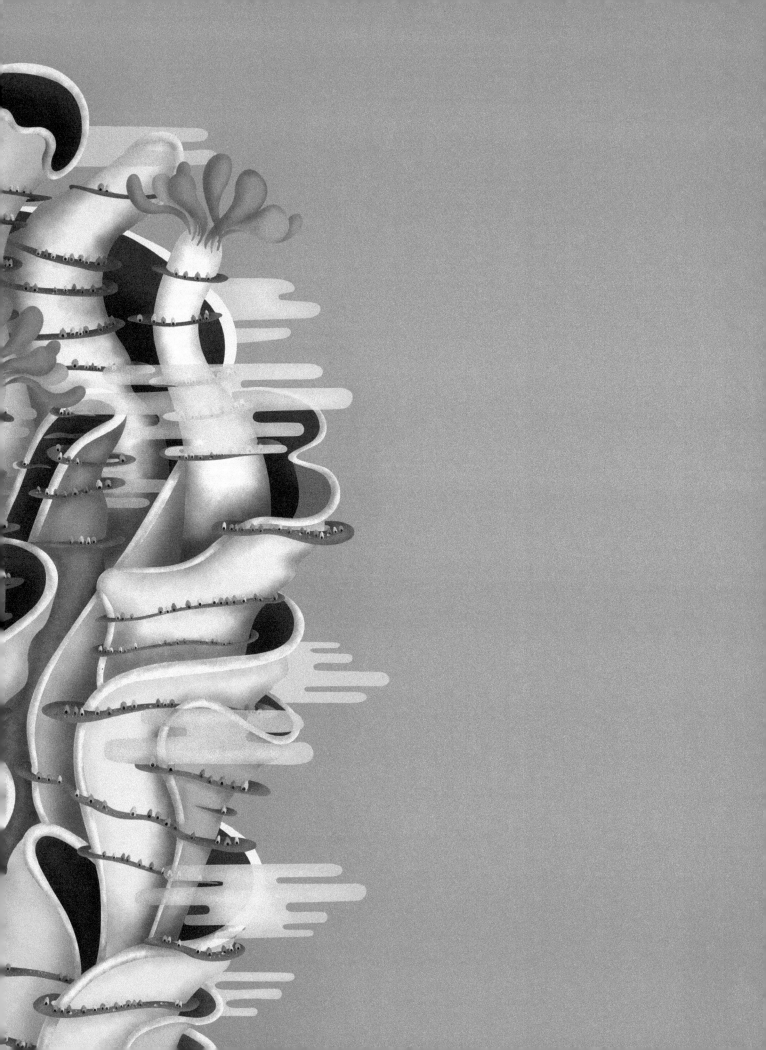

We liked to relax, play, dance and get shiny new things.

Most of all, we didn't care about our trash. All we knew was to throw it in the vast.

We have a market that sold
beautiful hats and capes.

We didn't mind not
knowing how they got
there in the first place.

We used the flowers on our
planet to make the hats and capes.

Loons would tell me my worries
for the flowers were wrong and
to pay them no mind.

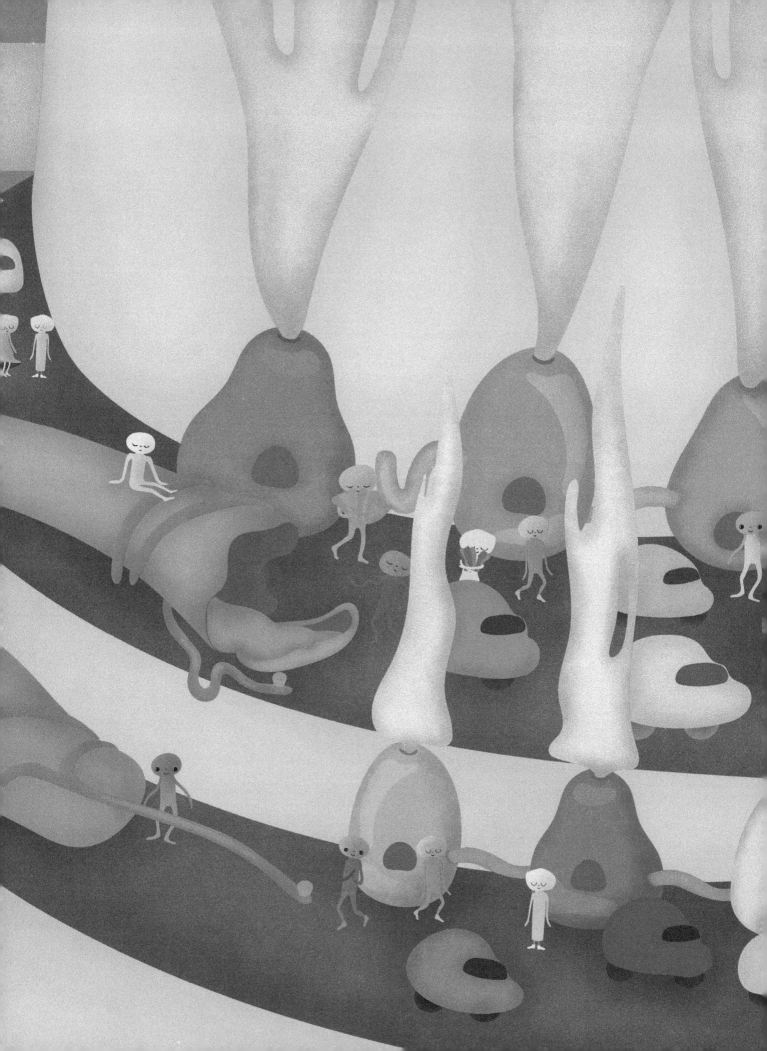

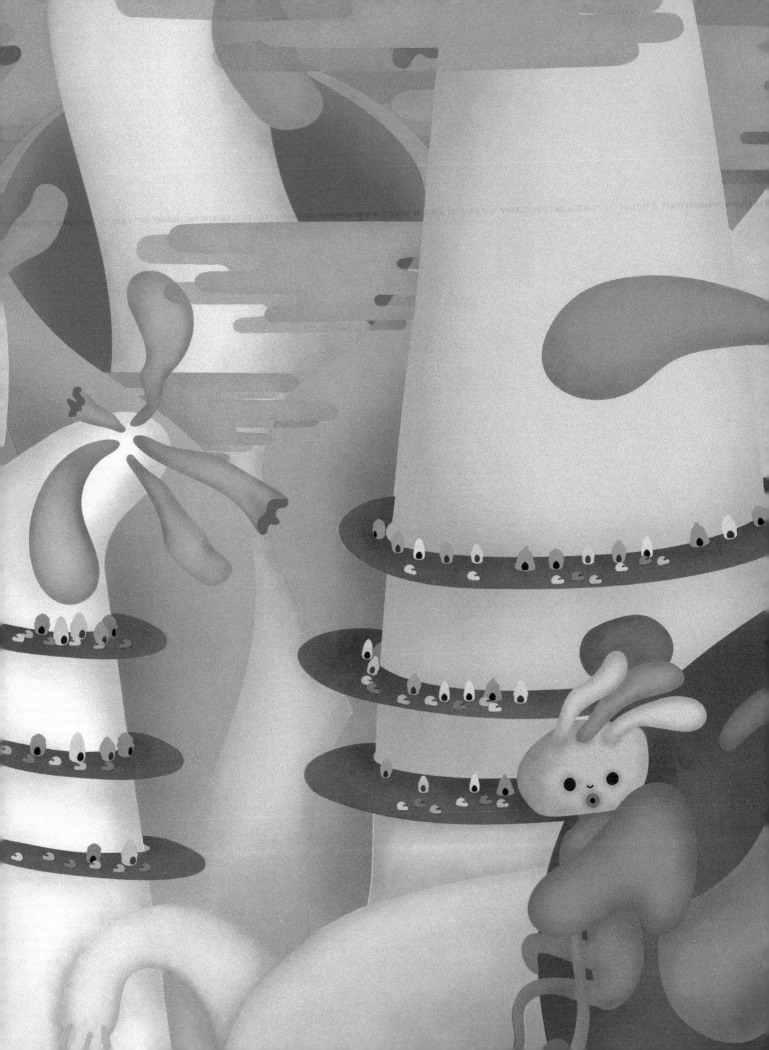

As Loons learned to make new things we started to care about ourselves way more always saying

ME ME ME!

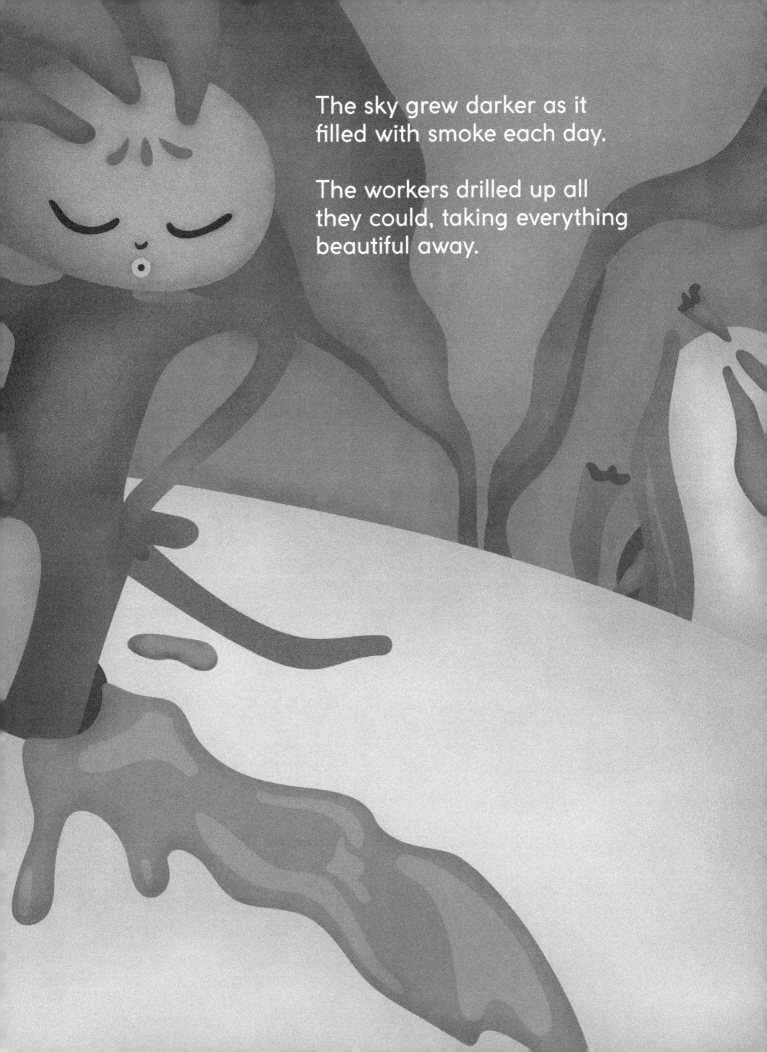

The sky grew darker as it filled with smoke each day.

The workers drilled up all they could, taking everything beautiful away.

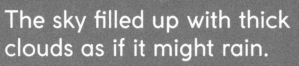

The sky filled up with thick
clouds as if it might rain.

We did not know what to
say as we watched our trash
overflow our pathways.

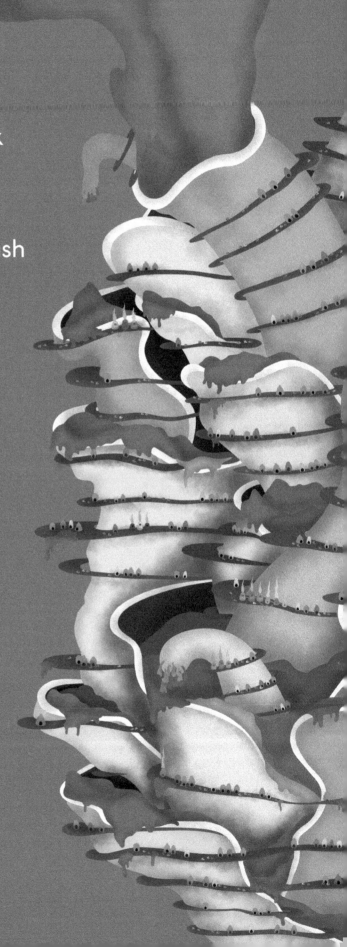

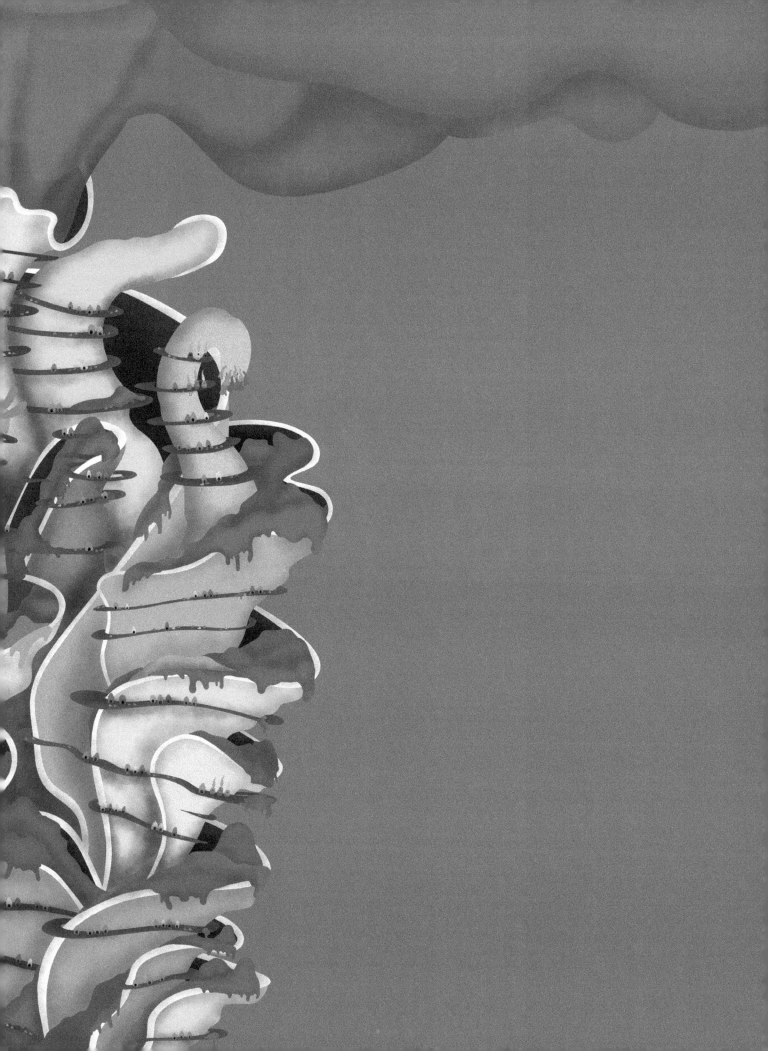

Our planet started to tremble
and shake.

We were shocked to see cracks
in our walls and our paths.

It rained heavier than ever – we felt really scared, but at least we had each other.

We huddled closely at home and watched the flooding start.

We didn't treat our planet with love and light, and for that, we knew our fears were right.

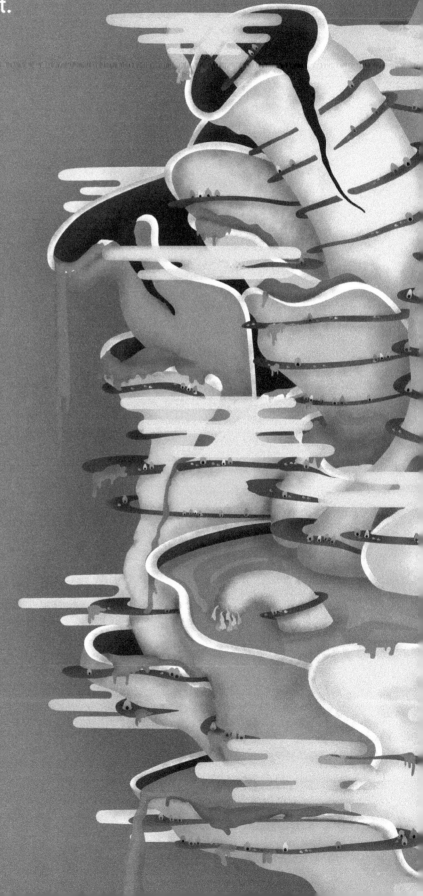

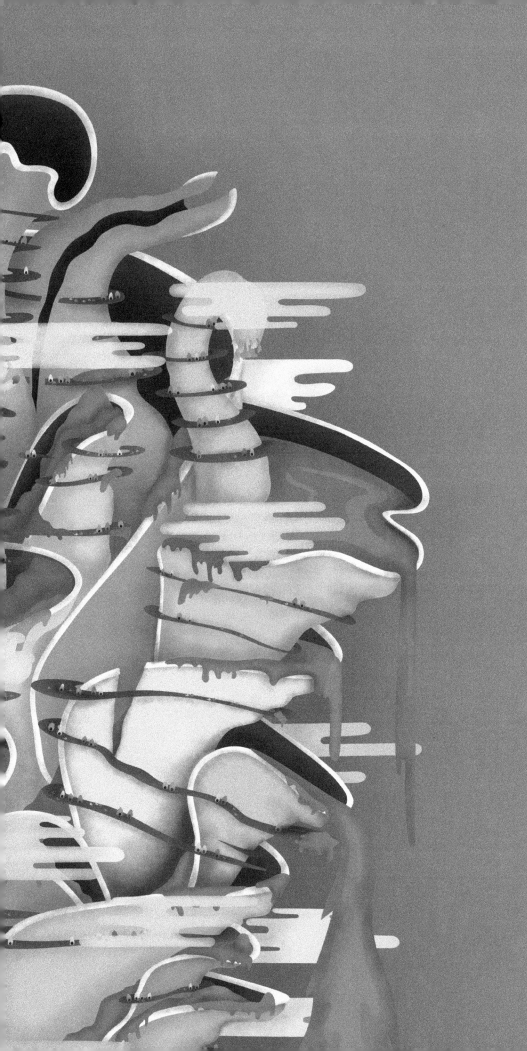

We knew we messed up and
didn't stop to think.

How could we have done this?

Our homes were gone due
to want and greed.

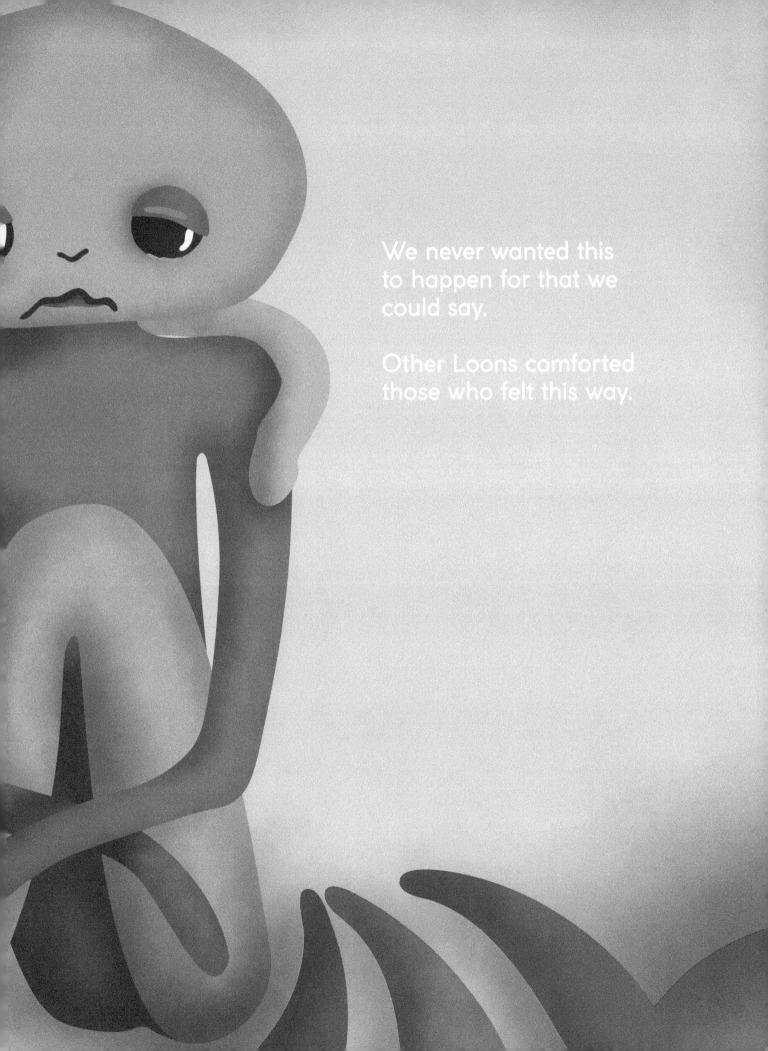

We never wanted this
to happen for that we
could say.

Other Loons comforted
those who felt this way.

We gathered our hats and capes and carried them to the water to stay.

As we walked, we found our loved ones along the way.

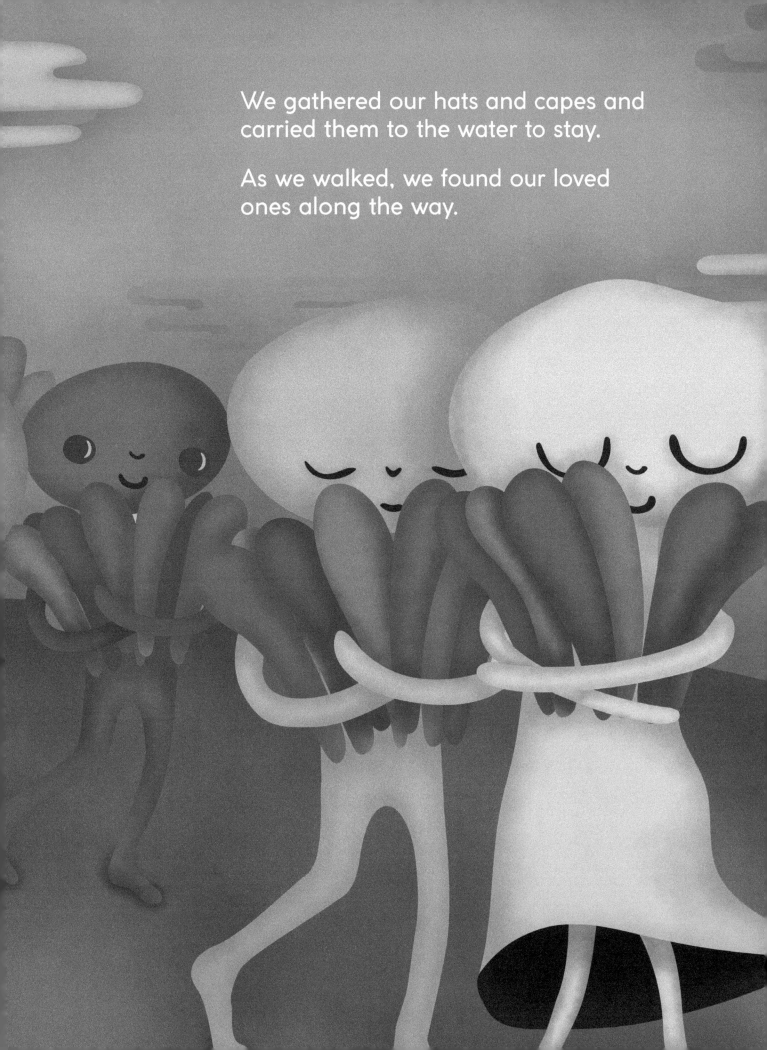

With time we started to see growth
little by little as we watched each day.

As our planet healed, we kept getting
happier that we got to stay.

We started to teach our little Loons about the past mistakes we made.

In hopes of making the future bright with unchanging loving ways.

We then come together to
celebrate and dance.

Everyone was thrilled and grateful
they got a second chance.

With passing time, we learned
that love and connection heals.

The loons had never been
happier, taking each day as a
new one to share and feel.

We learned to love our
planet neighbors and friends.

Most of all, we found peace
and purpose until the very end.

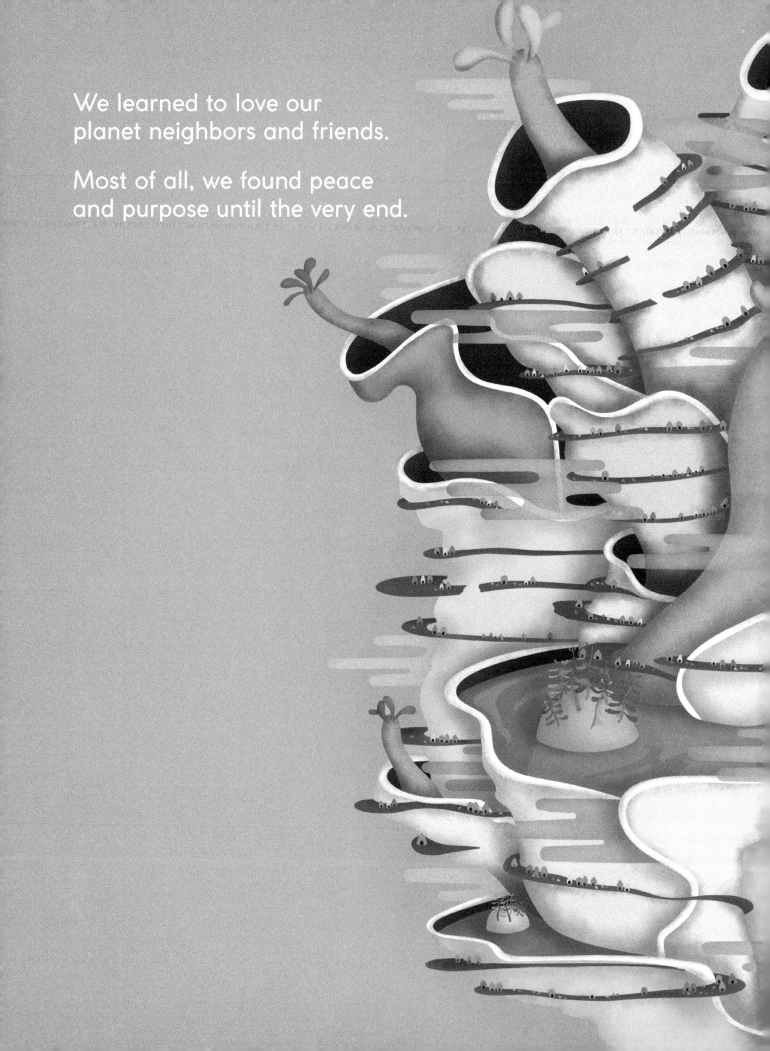

CPSIA information can be obtained
at www.ICGtesting.com
Printed in the USA
BVHW020443170720
583892BV00004B/52